The Night before Christmas

CLEMENT C. MOORE

The Night before Christmas

A Visit from St. Nicholas

ILLUSTRATED BY

MAX GROVER

BROWNDEER PRESS
HARCOURT BRACE & COMPANY
San Diego   New York   London

Requests for permission to make copies of any part of the work should be mailed to:
Permissions Department, Harcourt Brace & Company, 6277 Sea Harbor Drive, Orlando, Florida 32887-6777.

Browndeer Press is a registered trademark of Harcourt Brace & Company.

Library of Congress Cataloging-in-Publication Data
Moore, Clement Clarke, 1779–1863
The night before Christmas: a visit from St. Nicholas/Clement C. Moore; illustrated by Max Grover.
p. cm.
"Browndeer Press."
Summary: Presents the well-known poem about an important Christmas visitor.
ISBN 0-15-201713-5
1. Santa Claus— Juvenile poetry.   2. Christmas— Juvenile poetry.   3. Children's poetry, American.   [1. Santa Claus—Poetry.
2. Christmas—Poetry.   3. American poetry.   4. Narrative poetry.]   I. Grover, Max, ill.   II. Title.
PS2429.M5N5   1999
811'.2—dc21   98-15890

First edition
A C E F D B
Printed in Hong Kong

The illustrations in this book were done in acrylics on D'Arches Lavis Fedilis drawing paper.
The display type was set in Colwell.
The text type was set in Golden Original.
Color separations by Bright Arts Ltd., Hong Kong
Printed by South China Printing Company, Ltd., Hong Kong
This book was printed on totally chlorine-free Nymolla Matte Art paper.
Production supervision by Stanley Redfern and Pascha Gerlinger
Designed by Linda Lockowitz

Twas the night before Christmas,
when all through the house
Not a creature was stirring,
not even a mouse;
The stockings were hung
by the chimney with care,
In hopes that St. Nicholas
soon would be there;

The children were nestled
all snug in their beds,
While visions of sugar-plums
danced in their heads;
And Mamma in her 'kerchief,
and I in my cap,
Had just settled our brains
for a long winter's nap;

When out on the lawn
there arose such a clatter,
I sprang from the bed
to see what was the matter.
Away to the window
I flew like a flash,
Tore open the shutters
and threw up the sash.
The moon on the breast
of the new-fallen snow,
Gave the lustre of mid-day
to objects below,
When, what to my wondering eyes
should appear,

But a miniature sleigh,
and eight tiny rein-deer,
With a little old driver,
so lively and quick,
I knew in a moment
it must be St. Nick.

More rapid than eagles
his coursers they came,
And he whistled, and shouted,
and called them by name;
"Now, *Dasher!* now, *Dancer!*
now, *Prancer* and *Vixen!*
On, *Comet!* on, *Cupid!*
on, *Donder* and *Blitzen*!
To the top of the porch!
to the top of the wall!
Now dash away! dash away!
dash away all!"

As dry leaves that before
the wild hurricane fly,
When they meet with an obstacle,
mount to the sky;
So up to the house-top
the coursers they flew,
With the sleigh full of Toys,
and St. Nicholas too.

And then in a twinkling,
I heard on the roof,
The prancing and pawing
of each little hoof—
As I drew in my head,
and was turning around,
Down the chimney
St. Nicholas came with a bound.

He was dressed all in fur,
from his head to his foot,
And his clothes were all tarnished
with ashes and soot;
A bundle of Toys
he had flung on his back,
And he looked like a pedlar
just opening his pack.
His eyes—how they twinkled!
his dimples, how merry!
His cheeks were like roses,
his nose like a cherry!
His droll little mouth
was drawn up like a bow,

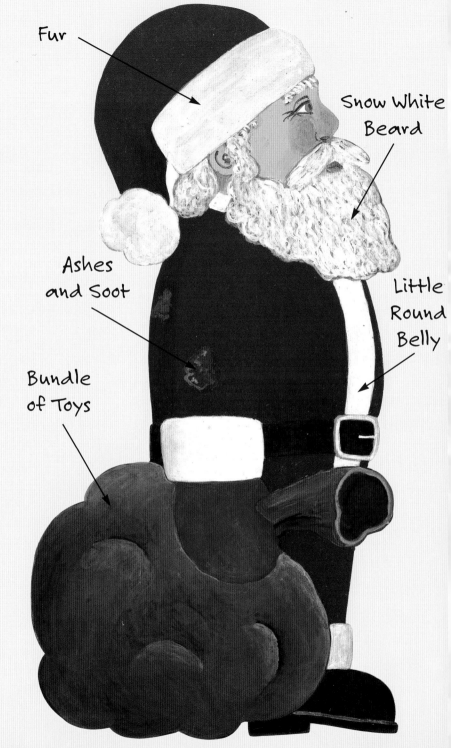

IDENTIFICATION CHART:

Fur

Snow White
Beard

Ashes
and Soot

Little
Round
Belly

Bundle
of Toys

How to Recognize Santa!

Twinkly Eyes

Rosy Cheeks

Dimples

Nose like a Cherry

Pipe

And the beard of his chin
was as white as the snow;
The stump of a pipe
he held tight in his teeth,
And the smoke it encircled
his head like a wreath;
He had a broad face
and a little round belly,
That shook when he laughed,
like a bowlfull of jelly.
He was chubby and plump,
a right jolly old elf,
And I laughed when I saw him,
in spite of myself,

A wink of his eye
and a twist of his head,
Soon gave me to know
I had nothing to dread;
He spoke not a word,
but went straight to his work,
And fill'd all the stockings;
then turned with a jerk,

And laying his finger
aside of his nose,
And giving a nod,
up the chimney he rose;

FOR santa

He sprang to his sleigh,
to his team gave a whistle,
And away they all flew
like the down of a thistle.
But I heard him exclaim,
ere he drove out of sight,

"HAPPY
CHRISTMAS
TO ALL . . .

AND TO ALL
A GOOD NIGHT."